SIMON & SCHUSTER BOOKS FOR YOUNG READERS
An imprint of Simon & Schuster Children's Publishing Division
1230 Avenue of the Americas, New York, New York 10020
SIMON & SCHUSTER BOOKS FOR YOUNG READERS is a trademark of Simon & Schuster, Inc.
For information about special discounts for bulk purchases, please contact Simon & Schuster Special Sales
at 1-866-506-1949 or business@simonandschuster.com.
The Simon & Schuster Speakers Bureau can bring authors to your live event.
For more information or to book an event, contact the Simon & Schuster Speakers Bureau
at 1-866-248-3049 or visit our website at www.simonspeakers.com.
The illustrations in this book were rendered in watercolor with digital tools.
Manufactured in China
0316 SCP • First Edition • 10 9 8 7 6 5 4 3 2 1
Library of Congress Cataloging-in-Publication Data
Miyares, Daniel, author, illustrator.
Bring me a rock! / Daniel Miyares.
pages cm
Summary: "A tiny insect king demands a rock with which to build his throne"—Provided by publisher.
ISBN 978-1-4814-4602-0 (hardcover)—ISBN 978-1-4814-4603-7 (eBook)
[1. Kings, queens, rulers, etc.—Fiction. 2. Ants—Fiction. 3. Humorous stories.] I. Title.
PZ7.M699577Bri 2016
[E]—dc23
2015016232

For Lisa, my rock

BRING ME A ROCK!

By Daniel Miyares

Simon & Schuster Books for Young Readers
New York London Toronto Sydney New Delhi

BRING ME A ROCK!

I WILL HAVE A MAJESTIC PEDESTAL FIT FOR A KING.

THAT'LL DO.

YAWN. NEXT, PLEASE.

IS THAT THE BEST YOU'VE GOT?

AT LAST, MY THRONE IS COMPLETE.

HELP!

What he needs...

is a pebble.

Bring me those rocks!